Carmela opened the box carefully. A snowy ball of cotton lay inside. As she pulled at the cotton, her fingers touched something hard and very small. She lifted a tiny silver rose on a fine chain.

"Oh, Tía Rosa. It's beautiful!" exclaimed Carmela.

"The Rose is so you'll remember your old Tía Rosa," she said.

"How could I forget you, Tía Rosa?" asked Carmela. "You're right here!"

You'll always be here, Carmela thought.

"The depiction of the strong sense of family and of coming to terms with death make this a good choice for all children."
—*School Library Journal*

"The author handles the subjects of grief and love very well.... [The] well-wrought pictures carry out the story's hopeful mood."
—*Booklist*

Other books of related interest
Ask your bookseller for the books you have
missed

ENCYCLOPEDIA BROWN,
    BOY DETECTIVE by Donald J. Sobol
FELITA by Nicholasa Mohr
MOLLY'S PILGRIM by Barbara Cohen
SONG OF THE TREES by Mildred D. Taylor
THE FRIENDSHIP and THE GOLD
    CADILLAC by Mildred D. Taylor
THANK YOU DR. MARTIN LUTHER
    KING, JR. by Eleanora E. Tate
MISSISSIPPI BRIDGE by Mildred D. Taylor
GOING HOME by Nicholasa Mohr
FRONT PORCH STORIES AT THE
    ONE-ROOM SCHOOL by Eleanora E. Tate
MAIZON AT BLUE HILL by Jacqueline Woodson

A Gift for Tía Rosa

by Karen T. Taha
Illustrated by Dee deRosa

A BANTAM SKYLARK BOOK
NEW YORK · TORONTO · LONDON · SYDNEY · AUCKLAND

This edition contains the complete text of the original hardcover edition.
NOT ONE WORD HAS BEEN OMITTED.

RL 2, 005–008

A GIFT FOR TÍA ROSA

A Bantam Skylark Book/published by arrangement with Macmillan, Inc.

PRINTING HISTORY
Dillon Press edition published 1986
Bantam edition/December 1991

Bantam Books are published by Bantam Books, a division of
Bantam Doubleday Dell Publishing Group, Inc. Its trade-
mark, consisting of the words "Bantam Books" and the
portrayal of a rooster, is Registered in U.S. Patent and
Trademark Office and in other countries. Marca Registrada.
Bantam Books, 1540 Broadway, New York, New York 10036.

PRINTED IN THE UNITED STATES OF AMERICA

CWO 0 9 8 7 6 5

In loving memory of
Frances Carver,
Aunt Fran

"AROUND, OVER, THROUGH, AND PULL. Around, over, through, and pull," Carmela repeated as she knitted. A rainbow of red, orange, and gold wool stretched almost to her feet. Now and then she stopped and listened for her father's car. He mustn't see what she was knitting!

The rumble of a motor made her drop the needles and run to the window. In the gray November shadows, she saw a battered brown station wagon turn into the garage next door.

"Mamá, she's home! Tía Rosa is home!" Carmela called. Carmela's mother hurried out of the bedroom. She put her arm around Carmela. They watched as lights flickered on in the windows, bringing the neat white house back to life.

"I know you want to see Tía Rosa, Carmela," said her mother, "but she and Tío Juan have had a long trip. Tía Rosa must be very tired after two weeks in the hospital."

"But can I call her, Mamá?" asked Carmela. "The scarf for Papá is almost done. She promised to help me fringe it when she came home."

"No, Carmela. Not now," her mother replied firmly. "Tía Rosa needs to rest." She smoothed back Carmela's thick black hair from her face.

Carmela tossed her head. "But Mamá . . . !"

"No, Carmela!"

Carmela knew there was no use arguing. But it wasn't fair. Tomorrow she would have to go to school. She couldn't see Tía Rosa until the afternoon. Her mother just didn't understand.

Frowning, Carmela plopped back on the sofa and picked up the silver

knitting needles. At least she would finish more of the scarf before Tía Rosa saw it tomorrow. She bent over her knitting and began once more. "Around, over, through, and pull." The phone rang in the kitchen.

"I'll get it!" Carmela shouted, bounding into the hall. "Hello?" Her dark eyes sparkled. "Tía Rosa! You must see Papá's scarf. It's almost finished . . . You did? For me? Okay, I'll be right there!"

The phone clattered as Carmela hung up. "Mamá! Tía Rosa wants to see the scarf. She even brought me a surprise!"

Carmela's mother smiled and shook her head. "Tía Rosa is unbelievable."

Carmela stuffed the bright wool into her school bag. "I'm going to make Tía Rosa a surprise after I finish Papá's scarf!" she called as she ran out.

She ran across the yard to Tía Rosa's front door. The door swung open, and there was Tío Juan. He looked taller and thinner than she remembered, and his eyes looked sad.

Tío Juan was as tall as Tía Rosa was short, Carmela thought. He was as thin as Tía Rosa was plump. And he was as good at listening as Tía Rosa was at talking.

"*Hola,* Carmelita," he said, bending to kiss her cheek. He led her down the hall. "Tía Rosa is sitting up in bed. She's tired, but she wanted to see her favorite neighbor."

Tía Rosa in bed! In all her eight years Carmela had never seen Tía Rosa sick. She held her breath and peeked into the bedroom. Tía Rosa's round face crinkled into a smile when she saw Carmela.

"Carmelita, come give me a hug!"

Hugging Tía Rosa always made Carmela feel safe and warm. Tía Rosa was like a soft pillow that smelled of soap and bath powder and sometimes of sweet tamales.

Now there was another smell, a dentist office smell, Carmela decided.

"Carmelita, I've missed you!" said Tía Rosa. "Let's look at what you have knitted."

Carmela handed her the scarf. Tía Rosa smiled. "Your papá will be proud to wear it," she said. "Tomorrow I'll show you how to fringe it, and I will start on the pink baby blanket for my granddaughter!"

Carmela laughed. "How do you know that Pepe's wife will have a girl?" she asked. Pepe was the oldest of Tía Rosa's six sons.

"Because," answered Tía Rosa with a grin, "anyone who has six sons and no daughters, deserves a grand-daughter!"

"But Tía Rosa, what if the baby is a boy? Won't you love him just the same?"

"Of course," laughed Tía Rosa. Carmela knew Tía Rosa would love the baby, boy or girl, but she crossed her fingers and wished for a girl, too.

"Now for the surprise!" said Tía Rosa. She handed Carmela a small white box. "Go on now. See what's inside."

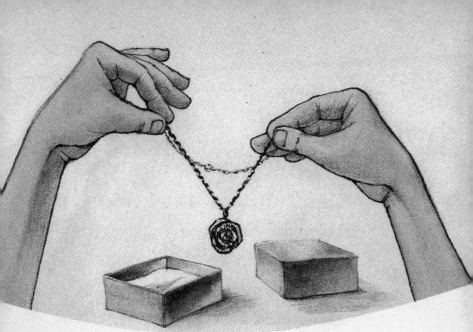

Carmela opened the box carefully. A snowy ball of cotton lay inside. As she pulled at the cotton, her fingers touched something hard and very small. She heard the "clish" of a chain as she lifted the surprise from under the cotton. In her hand Carmela held a tiny silver rose on a fine chain.

"Oh, Tía Rosa. It's beautiful!" exclaimed Carmela.

"The rose is so you'll remember your old Tía Rosa," she said.

"How could I forget you, Tía Rosa?" asked Carmela. "You're right here!"

Before she went home, Carmela put the rose around her neck. She promised to return the next day after school.

Carmela returned the next day, and the next, and every day for a whole week. Tía Rosa stayed in her room, and Tío Juan moved a chair by the bed for Carmela. Together the two friends worked on their surprise gifts.

"Why does Tía Rosa stay in bed all the time?" Carmela asked her father at breakfast one day.

Her father looked away for a moment. Then he took Carmela's hands in his. "Tía Rosa is very sick, Carmela. The doctors don't think she can get well," he explained.

"But Papá," said Carmela. "I have been sick lots of times. Remember when Tía Rosa stayed with me when you and Mama had to go away?"

"Yes," answered her father. "But

Tía Rosa . . ."

Carmela didn't listen. "Now I will stay with Tía Rosa until she gets well, too," she said.

Every afternoon Carmela worked on her father's scarf. The fringe was the easiest part. With Tía Rosa's help she would have the scarf finished long before Christmas.

Tía Rosa worked on the pink baby blanket, but the needles didn't fly in her sure brown fingers like they once did. Carmela teased her. "Tía

Rosa, are you knitting slowly because you might have to change the pink yarn to blue when the baby is born?"

"No, no," replied Tía Rosa with a grin. "The baby will surely be a girl. We need girls in this family. You're the only one I have!"

Sometimes Tía Rosa fell asleep with her knitting still in her hands.

Then Carmela would quietly put the needles and yarn into Tía Rosa's big green knitting bag and tiptoe out of the room.

Carmela liked Saturdays and Sundays best because she could spend more time at Tía Rosa's. Mamá always sent a plate of cookies with her, and Tío Juan made hot chocolate for them.

One Saturday morning when Carmela rang the doorbell, Tío Juan didn't come. Carmela ran to the garage and peeked in the window. The brown station wagon was gone.

She returned home and called Tía Rosa's number. The phone rang and rang. Carmela went down the steps to the basement. Her mother was rubbing stain into the freshly sanded wood of an old desk.

"Tía Rosa isn't home," said Carmela sadly. Her mother looked up from her work.

"I thought I heard a car in the night," said her mother. "Surely Tío Juan would have called us if . . ."

Just then the phone rang upstairs. Carmela heard footsteps creak across the floor as her father walked to answer it.

Moments later the footsteps thumped softly toward the basement door. Carmela's father came slowly down the steps. Carmela shivered when she saw his sad face. He put his arms around Carmela and her mother and hugged them close. "Tía Rosa is gone," he whispered. "She died early this morning."

No, her father's words couldn't be true. Carmela didn't believe it. Tía Rosa would come back. She had

always come back before.

"It's not true!" cried Carmela. She broke away from her mother and father and raced up the stairs. She ran out the front door and through the yard to Tía Rosa's house. She pushed the doorbell again and again. She pounded on the silent door until her fists hurt. At last she sank down on the steps.

Later her father came. With a soft hanky he brushed the tears from her cheeks. At last they walked quietly home.

The next days were long and lonely for Carmela. She didn't care that Papá's finished scarf lay hidden in her closet, bright and beautiful. She didn't want to see it. She didn't want to feel the cool, smooth knitting needles in her hands ever again.

The white house next door was busy with people coming and going. Carmela took over food her mother and father cooked, but she quickly returned home. She didn't like to see Tío Juan. Seeing Tío Juan made her miss Tía Rosa even more.

One day Carmela said to her

mother, "Tía Rosa died before I could give her anything, Mamá. She baked me cookies and taught me to knit and brought me surprises. I was going to surprise her. Now it's too late."

"Carmela, Tía Rosa didn't want her kindness returned. She wanted it passed on," said her mother. "That way a part of Tía Rosa will never die."

"But I wanted to give something to her!" shouted Carmela. "Just to Tía Rosa. To show her that I loved her!"

"She knew that, Carmela. Every smile and hug and visit told her that you loved her," said her mother. "Now it's Tío Juan who needs our love."

"I know," answered Carmela in a soft voice, "but it's hard, Mamá. It hurts so much without Tía Rosa."

One night Carmela's mother asked Tío Juan to dinner. Carmela met him at the door. This time Carmela did not turn away when she saw his sad eyes. Instead, she hugged him tightly.

For the first time in a week, Tío

Juan smiled. "Carmelita, tomorrow you must come next door. I would like you to meet my new grand-daughter. Her parents have named her Rosita, little Rose, after her grandmother."

Carmela looked down at her silver rose necklace so Tío Juan would not see the tears in her eyes. Tía Rosa knew the baby would be a girl. Then Carmela remembered the unfin-ished blanket. "Now I know what I can give!" she said.

After dinner Tío Juan went back to the white house. A few minutes later he returned with Tía Rosa's big

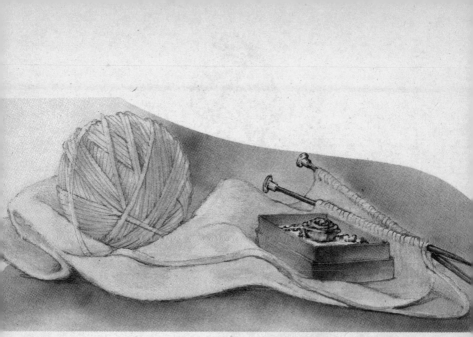

knitting bag. Very carefully Carmela pulled out the half-finished blanket and wound the soft pink yarn around the needle.

"Around, over, through, and pull. Around, over, through, and pull." Carmela smiled. At last she had a gift for Tía Rosa.

ABOUT THE AUTHOR

KAREN T. TAHA is a library media specialist in Springdale, Arkansas. She holds two master's degrees, one in Spanish and one in instructional resources.

Ms. Taha has published several short stories. *A Gift for Tía Rosa* is her first novel.

Ms. Taha is a world traveler, having lived in Spain, Egypt, and Mexico. She and her family have also lived in Kuwait for a year.

ABOUT THE ILLUSTRATOR

DEE DEROSA has illustrated a number of books for young readers. She lives in Syracuse, New York.